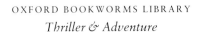

OXFORD BOOKWORMS LIBRARY
Thriller & Adventure

The Fifteenth Character

Starter (250 headwords)

ROSEMARY BORDER

The Fifteenth Character

Illustrated by
David Hine

OXFORD UNIVERSITY PRESS

OXFORD

UNIVERSITY PRESS

Great Clarendon Street, Oxford OX2 6DP

Oxford University Press is a department of the University of Oxford.
It furthers the University's objective of excellence in research, scholarship,
and education by publishing worldwide in

Oxford New York

Auckland Cape Town Dar es Salaam Hong Kong Karachi
Kuala Lumpur Madrid Melbourne Mexico City Nairobi
New Delhi Shanghai Taipei Toronto

With offices in

Argentina Austria Brazil Chile Czech Republic France Greece
Guatemala Hungary Italy Japan Poland Portugal Singapore
South Korea Switzerland Thailand Turkey Ukraine Vietnam

OXFORD and OXFORD ENGLISH are registered trade marks of
Oxford University Press in the UK and in certain other countries

ISBN: 978 0 19 423421 4

A complete recording of this Bookworms edition of
The Fifteenth Character is available on audio CD. ISBN 978 0 19 423403 0

Printed in China

Word count (main text): 1400

For more information on the Oxford Bookworms Library, visit
www.oup.com/bookworms

CONTENTS

1
JOBS FOR TODAY

Every day lots of different people come to Happy Hills because there are lots of exciting things to do.

Sally Brown works at Happy Hills in her holiday. She is a student and she wants to be a teacher.

'I need the money,' she tells her family, 'and it's an interesting job.' But she is always very tired in the evening.

The workers at Happy Hills arrive early in the morning. They all wear clean green trousers and yellow shirts. They must smile a lot and be nice to all the visitors.

Every morning Mr Parry puts a list of *Jobs for Today* in the workers' canteen. Mr Parry wears different clothes. His shirt is green and his trousers are white, and he wears a red coat with *I'm Ken Parry. Can I help you?* on his pocket. The visitors call him Ken, but all the workers call him Mr Parry.

Today Sally arrives at Happy Hills at eight o'clock. On her shirt there is a picture of a smiling face and *Have a Happy Day* in black and red writing. She goes to the canteen and looks for Mr Parry's list.

'What job am I doing today?' Sally thinks. 'Am I making tea, or helping in the children's play house?'

But Sally is wrong. The list says, 'Sally Brown – Connie Cat. Break: eleven o'clock.'

'Oh no!' thinks Sally. Nobody likes wearing the costumes. But at Happy Hills the characters are very important. The visitors like to take photos of their children with Cowboy Joe, Charlie Clown, Baby Blue Eyes, Photo Phil, Big John, Connie Cat, Big Apple, Miss Flower, Edward Elephant and all their friends.

Everybody always asks the same questions, 'Are you very hot in your costume?' and 'How do you eat and drink?'

Edward Elephant has the best job. He has a bag of water under his costume. He can spray the visitors with water. And Photo Phil and Charlie Clown make everybody laugh. But Connie Cat cannot do that. She can only say *miaow* to the children all day.

Sally looks for her costume. A tall man in a cowboy costume is standing beside her.

'Hullo, Sally,' says the cowboy. 'It's me – William.' William is a student too. He is Sally's friend. 'Which costume are you looking for?'

'Connie Cat. When's your break?'

'Eleven o'clock.'

'Me too.'

2
HERE COMES ZAPP!

It is nine o'clock. The doors open, but there are not many visitors today. They all have invitations and they show them to Mr Parry. A very famous man is coming to Happy Hills, so Mr Parry is very excited.

'Zapp's coming today. He's opening the new Zapp-o-copter,' says William to Sally.

'Stop talking and do some work!' says Mr Parry.

Zapp is a singer. Sally loves listening to his songs and she has all his CDs. There is a picture of him in her room too.

The Zapp-o-copter is very exciting. People can sit in little helicopters and go up and down very fast. The visitors stand behind a blue rope and wait for Zapp.

'Please stay behind the rope,' says Mr Parry.

Suddenly there is a noise in the sky. Everybody looks up.

'It's Zapp's helicopter!' says William.

The helicopter comes down and Zapp gets out. He smiles at the visitors.

'Oh – he's wonderful!' says a young girl. She gives Zapp a flower. He gives her a big smile and says, 'Thank you'.

Sally is hot and thirsty in her costume. She wants to talk too, but Mr Parry is watching.

3
ZAPP'S NEW SONG

Mr Parry takes the singer to the Zapp-o-copter. Zapp cuts the rope.

'Thank you, Zapp. Now please can you sing for us?' says Mr Parry.

'OK! But the people must help me!' he says. He begins to sing. Everybody knows the song and sings it with him.

'Thank you,' says Zapp. You're all wonderful singers. Now look at this.' He takes a CD out of his pocket. 'This is my new song,' he says.

'Please sing it for us!' say the TV men. But Zapp smiles. 'No, no – you must come to my big concert next Saturday.' He puts the CD in his pocket again.

'Now let's go on the Zapp-o-copter!' says Zapp. He sees a teacher with some children. 'Would they like to come too?' he asks her. 'Of course,' says the teacher. They help the children into the helicopters.

Zapp smiles and smiles. The photographers take lots of pictures. Photo Phil arrives too. He is one of the Happy Hills characters. He takes a photo of the children – and sprays them with water! Everybody laughs.

Zapp is having a wonderful day. He speaks to the TV people. The photographers take photos of him with all the characters. Zapp meets Charlie Clown. Charlie gives him a flower – and the flower sprays him with water. Everybody laughs.

Sally meets Zapp too, and she is very excited. But she cannot talk to him because she is wearing her cat costume and Mr Parry is watching.

4
WHERE'S ZAPP'S CD?

'Come on, it's eleven o'clock,' says William. 'Let's go to the canteen for our break. We've got ten minutes.'

They sit down in the canteen and take off their heads. Sally is thirsty. Her face is hot and red. William is hot and thirsty too. They have a long drink of cold water. 'That's good!' William says. Then he looks at his watch. 'Ten past eleven,' he says. 'Come on, Sally. Back to work!'

They finish their drinks and put their heads on again.

Suddenly a lot of people come into the canteen.

'What's the matter?' says William.

'Zapp's CD!' says Mr Parry. 'He can't find it!'

Everybody is unhappy, but Zapp is angry too.

 'That CD's important, Parry,' he says. 'You must find it.'

 'I'm doing my best, Zapp,' says Mr Parry. 'Don't hit me, please – I'm doing my best!'

A lot of things happen very quickly. The visitors want to go home, but suddenly Mr Parry closes all the doors.

'Nobody can leave,' he says. 'I'm sorry, but Zapp's CD's very important and we must find it.'

Mr Parry makes a telephone call. Very soon four police arrive in a big white police car. They ask a lot of questions.

The police look everywhere for the CD. They read Mr Parry's list of visitors. They count the visitors carefully and look in all their pockets and bags.

There is a lot of noise. People are angry and tired. They want to go home now. And Zapp is speaking very quietly into a little black telephone. Photo Phil goes to him and says, 'Smile, please!'

'Go away!' says Zapp angrily.

Now the police want to talk to the workers. One stays with the visitors and three police speak to the workers in the canteen. Zapp comes with the police.

'You must find that CD!' says Zapp.

'We're doing our best, Zapp,' say the police.

5

THE FIFTEENTH CHARACTER

Sally waits quietly with the other workers. She looks at Mr Parry's *Jobs for Today* list and counts the names.

There are twenty-nine names on the list today. Fifteen people are *helpers*. They wear green trousers and yellow shirts and help the visitors. Fourteen people are *characters* and wear costumes.

JOBS FOR TODAY

Maggie Street - Edward Elephant
William Johnson - Cowboy Joe
Anna Harris - Cowgirl Flo
Sally Brown - Connie Cat
Eddy White - Big Apple
Sam Wilson - Sir Laugh-a-Lot
Zara Anderson - Lady Love-a-Little
John Carr - Photo Phil
Joe Robinson - Willy
Sharon May - Milly
Mike Smith - Larry Longlegs
Polly Wells - Blue Bird
Frank Pooley - Don Driver
Dan Donovan - Baby Blue Eyes

'Wait a minute,' thinks Sally. 'There are fourteen characters on the list. But there are fifteen characters here!'

She reads the list again, very, very carefully. 'Edward Elephant – yes, he's here. Connie Cat – that's me. Cowboy Joe – that's William. Photo Phil – yes, he's here. Big Apple – yes. Sir Laugh-a-Lot and Lady Love-a-Little . . . Wait a minute, Charlie Clown isn't on the list – but Charlie's *here* in this room!'

21

'Excuse me, Mr Parry,' says Sally. 'There are fourteen characters on your list, but there are fifteen in the room now. Charlie Clown isn't on the list, but he's here.'

Mr Parry reads the list and counts the characters. 'You're right, Sally,' he says.

'Take off your heads!' Mr Parry says to the characters.

They take off their heads.

Charlie Clown is a woman.

'Why are you wearing that costume?' asks Mr Parry.

The woman begins to run away, but William stops her.

The police take off her costume – and find a big pocket. In it they find Zapp's CD. The singer smiles again.

It is Saturday night. Sally and William are in London because they are going to Zapp's concert. There are lots of excited people and TV photographers outside the hall. Everybody wants to hear Zapp's new song.

'Where are your tickets?' says the man at the door to Sally.

'We haven't got any tickets,' says Sally. The man begins to look angry. Sally smiles and takes something out of her pocket. 'Is this invitation OK? It's from Zapp.'

GLOSSARY

break a time when people can stop work to have tea or coffee

canteen a room where workers eat and drink

character a person or animal in a story or film

concert a time when someone plays or sings in a big room for a lot of people

costume special clothes

count *(vb)* number objects or people

famous *(adj)* someone who many people know is famous

hall a big room where someone sings or plays music for a lot of people

holiday a time when we do not go to work

invitation a letter asking someone to come to a party or concert

job work that people do for money

list a lot of names on a piece of paper

miaow the sound a cat makes

pocket a place in your shirt or trousers where you can put things

song something that people sing

spray send out water through the air

The Fifteenth Character

ACTIVITIES

Before Reading

1 Look at the front cover of the book. Now complete these sentences.

  1 This story happens . . .
   a ☐ in the future.
   b ☐ in today's world.
   c ☐ sometime long ago.
  2 The character looks . . .
   a ☐ frightening.
   b ☐ exciting.
   c ☐ funny.

2 Read the back cover of the book. Guess the answers to these questions.

  1 What is Happy Hills?
  2 What does Sally do?
  3 What goes wrong?
  4 Is Zapp a man or a woman?

While Reading

1 Read pages 1–4.
Are these sentences true (T) or false (F)?

		T	F
1	Sally Brown is a student.	☐	☐
2	The workers at Happy Hills must wear white shirts and red trousers.	☐	☐
3	Sally always puts a list of *Jobs for Today* in the canteen.	☐	☐
4	The visitors like to take photos of their children with the Happy Hills characters.	☐	☐

2 Read pages 5–8, then match the sentences halves to make five complete sentences.

1 Sally works at Happy Hills . . .
2 Edward Elephant has the best job . . .
3 Mr Parry is excited . . .
4 William is wearing a cowboy costume . . .
5 Sally has a picture of Zapp in her room . . .

a because today he is Cowboy Joe.
b because a very famous man is coming to Happy Hills.
c because she loves his songs.
d because she needs the money.
e because he can spray the visitors with water.

3 **Read pages 9–12.**
  Are these sentences true (T) or false (F)?

		T	F
1	Zapp comes to Happy Hills in a helicopter.	☐	☐
2	Zapp sings his new song.	☐	☐
3	The photographers take lots of pictures of Zapp with the characters.	☐	☐
4	Zapp smiles and smiles.	☐	☐

4 **Read pages 13–16, then join the sentences with *and* or *because*.**

  1 Charlie Clown gives Zapp a flower. The flower sprays him with water.
  2 Sally can't talk to Zapp. She is wearing her cat costume.
  3 Sally is thirsty. Her face is hot and red.

5 **Read pages 17–21. Who says or thinks these sentences?**

  1 'Nobody can leave.'
  2 'Smile please!'
  3 'You must find that CD!'
  4 'Wait a minute . . . There are fifteen characters here!'

6 **Read pages 22–24, then answer these questions.**

  1 Where do the policemen find Zapp's CD?
  2 Who stops the girl?
  3 Where do Sally and William go on Saturday night?
  4 Why don't they need tickets?

After Reading

1 Put these twelve sentences in the right order to tell the story.

a ☐1☐ Sally comes to work and looks at *Jobs for Today*.

b ☐ 'Take off your heads!' Mr Parry tells the characters.

c ☐ Zapp tells everybody about his new CD.

d ☐ Zapp arrives in a red helicopter.

e ☐ Mr Parry runs into the canteen. 'Zapp can't find his CD!' he says.

f ☐ Sally counts the characters. 'There are fourteen characters on the list,' she says, 'but there are fifteen characters here!'

g ☐ The singer cuts the rope and opens the Zapp-o-copter.

h ☐ Zapp gives Sally an invitation to his big concert.

i ☐ Today Sally is Connie Cat and her friend William is Cowboy Joe.

j ☐ Charlie Clown gives Zapp a flower – and the flower sprays him with water.

k ☐ Four policemen arrive and ask a lot of questions.

l ☐ The policemen find the CD in Charlie Clown's pocket.

2 Choose the right words for each picture. Write a letter in each box.

1    The children are saying: ☐

2    The police are saying: ☐

3    Sally is saying: ☐

4    The policewoman is saying: ☐

a 'What have you got in your pockets, please?'
b 'This is exciting!'
c 'Come on – you're coming with us.'
d 'Is this invitation OK? It's from Zapp.'

ABOUT THE AUTHOR

Rosemary Border is a very experienced teacher and writer. She has also worked as an editor, a lawyer, and a journalist. She is the author of many books for learners of English – more than she can remember. 'I stopped counting after 150,' she says. She has written and retold more than eighty graded readers, including many stories for the Oxford Bookworms Library. These include *Drive into Danger* (Starter, Thriller & Adventure) and *The Lottery Winner* (Stage 1, Human Interest).

OXFORD BOOKWORMS LIBRARY

Classics • Crime & Mystery • Factfiles • Fantasy & Horror
Human Interest • Playscripts • Thriller & Adventure
True Stories • World Stories

The OXFORD BOOKWORMS LIBRARY provides enjoyable reading in English, with a wide range of classic and modern fiction, non-fiction, and plays. It includes original and adapted texts in seven carefully graded language stages, which take learners from beginner to advanced level. An overview is given on the next pages.

All Stage 1 titles are available as audio recordings, as well as over eighty other titles from Starter to Stage 6. All Starters and many titles at Stages 1 to 4 are specially recommended for younger learners. Every Bookworm is illustrated, and Starters and Factfiles have full-colour illustrations.

The OXFORD BOOKWORMS LIBRARY also offers extensive support. Each book contains an introduction to the story, notes about the author, a glossary, and activities. Additional resources include tests and worksheets, and answers for these and for the activities in the books. There is advice on running a class library, using audio recordings, and the many ways of using Oxford Bookworms in reading programmes. Resource materials are available on the website <www.oup.com/bookworms>.

The *Oxford Bookworms Collection* is a series for advanced learners. It consists of volumes of short stories by well-known authors, both classic and modern. Texts are not abridged or adapted in any way, but carefully selected to be accessible to the advanced student.

You can find details and a full list of titles in the *Oxford Bookworms Library Catalogue* and *Oxford English Language Teaching Catalogues*, and on the website <www.oup.com/bookworms>.

THE OXFORD BOOKWORMS LIBRARY
GRADING AND SAMPLE EXTRACTS

STARTER • 250 HEADWORDS

present simple – present continuous – imperative –
can/cannot, must – going to (future) – simple gerunds …

Her phone is ringing – but where is it?

Sally gets out of bed and looks in her bag. No phone. She looks under the bed. No phone. Then she looks behind the door. There is her phone. Sally picks up her phone and answers it. *Sally's Phone*

STAGE 1 • 400 HEADWORDS

… past simple – coordination with *and, but, or* –
subordination with *before, after, when, because, so* …

I knew him in Persia. He was a famous builder and I worked with him there. For a time I was his friend, but not for long. When he came to Paris, I came after him – I wanted to watch him. He was a very clever, very dangerous man. *The Phantom of the Opera*

STAGE 2 • 700 HEADWORDS

… present perfect – *will* (future) – *(don't) have to, must not, could* –
comparison of adjectives – simple *if* clauses – past continuous –
tag questions – *ask/tell* + infinitive …

While I was writing these words in my diary, I decided what to do. I must try to escape. I shall try to get down the wall outside. The window is high above the ground, but I have to try. I shall take some of the gold with me – if I escape, perhaps it will be helpful later. *Dracula*

… should, may – present perfect continuous – *used to* – past perfect –
causative – relative clauses – indirect statements …

Of course, it was most important that no one should see
Colin, Mary, or Dickon entering the secret garden. So Colin
gave orders to the gardeners that they must all keep away
from that part of the garden in future. **The Secret Garden**

STAGE 4 • 1400 HEADWORDS

… past perfect continuous – passive (simple forms) –
would conditional clauses – indirect questions –
relatives with *where/when* – gerunds after prepositions/phrases …

I was glad. Now Hyde could not show his face to the world
again. If he did, every honest man in London would be proud
to report him to the police. **Dr Jekyll and Mr Hyde**

STAGE 5 • 1800 HEADWORDS

… future continuous – future perfect –
passive (modals, continuous forms) –
would have conditional clauses – modals + perfect infinitive …

If he had spoken Estella's name, I would have hit him. I was so
angry with him, and so depressed about my future, that I could
not eat the breakfast. Instead I went straight to the old house.
Great Expectations

STAGE 6 • 2500 HEADWORDS

… passive (infinitives, gerunds) – advanced modal meanings –
clauses of concession, condition

When I stepped up to the piano, I was confident. It was as if I
knew that the prodigy side of me really did exist. And when I
started to play, I was so caught up in how lovely I looked that
I didn't worry how I would sound. **The Joy Luck Club**

Drive into Danger

ROSEMARY BORDER

'I can drive a truck,' says Kim on her first day at work in the office. When Kim's passenger Andy finds something strange under the truck things get dangerous – very dangerous.

Orca

PHILLIP BURROWS AND MARK FOSTER

When Tonya and her friends decide to sail around the world they want to see exciting things and visit exciting places.

But one day, they meet an orca – a killer whale – one of the most dangerous animals in the sea. And life gets a little too exciting.

Mystery in London

HELEN BROOKE

Six women are dead because of the Whitechapel Killer. Now another woman lies in a London street and there is blood everywhere. She is very ill. You are the famous detective Mycroft Pound; can you catch the killer before he escapes?

The Ransom of Red Chief

O. HENRY

Retold by Paul Shipton

Bill and Sam arrive in the small American town of Summit with only two hundred dollars, but they need more and Sam has an idea for making a lot of money. When things start to go very wrong, both men soon regret their visit – and the idea.

BOOKWORMS · HUMAN INTEREST · STAGE 1

The Lottery Winner

ROSEMARY BORDER

Everybody wants to win the lottery. A million pounds, perhaps five million, even ten million. How wonderful! Emma Carter buys a ticket for the lottery every week, and puts the ticket carefully in her bag. She is seventy-three years old and does not have much money. She would like to visit her son in Australia, but aeroplane tickets are very expensive.

Jason Williams buys lottery tickets every week too. But he is not a very nice young man. He steals things. He hits old ladies in the street, snatches their bags and runs away . . .

BOOKWORMS · FANTASY & HORROR · STAGE 1

The Wizard of Oz

L. FRANK BAUM

Retold by Rosemary Border

Dorothy lives in Kansas, USA, but one day a cyclone blows her and her house to a strange country called Oz. There, Dorothy makes friends with the Scarecrow, the Tin Man, and the Cowardly Lion.

But she wants to go home to Kansas. Only one person can help her, and that is the country's famous Wizard. So Dorothy and her friends take the yellow brick road to the Emerald City, to find the Wizard of Oz . . .